KU-181-306

SOUTHWARK LIBRARIES
SK 2672741 2

HORRID HENRY
and the Zombie Vampire

HORRID HENRY and the Zombie Vampire

Francesca Simon
Illustrated by Tony Ross

Orion
Children's Books

Horrid Henry and the Zombie Vampire was first published
in the story book of the same name
First published in Great Britain in 2011 by Orion Children's Books
This edition first published in Great Britain in 2018
by Hodder and Stoughton

1 3 5 7 9 10 8 6 4 2

A CIP catalogue record for this book
is available from the British Library.

ISBN 978 1 5101 0202 6

Printed and bound in China

The paper and board used in this book are from well-managed forests
and other responsible sources.

Orion Children's Books
An imprint of
Hachette Children's Group
Part of Hodder and Stoughton
Carmelite House
50 Victoria Embankment
London EC4Y 0DZ

An Hachette UK Company
www.hachette.co.uk
www.hachettechildrens.co.uk
www.horridhenry.co.uk

To Professor Eric Stanley,
inspiring teacher and great friend

There are many more
Horrid Henry Early Reader books available.

For a complete list visit:
www.horridhenry.co.uk

Contents

Chapter 1

'Isn't it exciting, Henry?' said Perfect Peter, packing Bunnykins carefully in his Sammy the Snail overnight bag. 'A museum sleepover! With a torch-lit trail! And worksheets! I can't think of anything more fun.'

'I can,' snarled Horrid Henry. Being trapped in a cave with Clever Clare reciting all the multiplication tables from one to a million.

Watching *Cooking Cuties*. Even visiting Nurse Needle for one of her horrible injections. (Well, maybe not *that*).

But *almost* anything would be better than being stuck overnight in Our Town Museum on a class sleepover. No TV. No computers. No comics.

Why oh why did he have to do this?

He wanted to sleep in his own comfy bed, not in a sleeping bag on the museum's cold hard floor, surrounded by photos of old mayors and a few dusty exhibits.

AAARRRRRGGGHH.

Wasn't it bad enough he was bored all day in school without being bored all night too?

Worse, Peter's nappy baby class was coming, too. They'd probably have to be tucked in at seven o'clock, when they'd all start crying for their mamas. Ugghh.

And then Miss Battle-Axe snarling at them to finish their worksheets, and Moody Margaret snoring and Anxious Andrew whimpering that he'd seen a ghost . . .

Well, no way was he going to that boring old dump without some comics to pass the time. He'd just bought the latest *Screamin' Demon* with a big article all about vampires and zombies. Yay! He couldn't wait to read it.

Perfect Peter watched him stuff his Mutant Max bag full of comics. 'Henry, you know we're not allowed to bring comics to the museum sleepover,' said Perfect Peter.

'Shut up and mind your own business, toad,' said Horrid Henry.

'Mum! Henry just called me a toad!' wailed Peter. 'And he told me to shut up.'

'Toady Toady Toady, Toady Toady Toady,' jeered Henry.

'Henry! Stop being horrid or no museum sleepover for you,' yelled Mum.

Horrid Henry paused. Was it too late to be horrid enough to get banned from the sleepover? Why hadn't he thought of this before? Why, he could . . .

'Henry! Peter! We have to leave now!' yelled Dad.

Rats.

Chapter 2

The children queued up in the museum's Central Hall clutching their sleeping bags as Miss Lovely and Miss Battle-Axe ticked off names on a big register.

'Go away, Susan,' said Moody Margaret. 'After what you did at my house I'm going to sit with Gurinder. So there.'

'You're such a meanie, Margaret,' said Sour Susan.

'Am not.'

'Are too.'

Susan scowled. Margaret was *always* so mean. If only she could think of a way to pay that old grouch back.

Margaret scowled. Susan was *always* so annoying. If only she could think of a way to pay that old fraidy cat back.

Henry scowled. Why did he have to be here? What he'd give for a magic carpet to whisk him straight home to the comfy black chair to watch *Terminator Gladiator.*

Could life get any worse?

'Henwy,' came a little voice next to him. 'I love you Henwy. I want to give you a big kiss.'

Oh no, thought Horrid Henry. Oh no. It was Lisping Lily, New Nick's little sister. What was that foul fiend doing here?

'You keep away from me,' said Horrid Henry, pushing and shoving his way through the children to escape her.

'Waaa!' wept Weepy William as Henry stepped on his foot.

'I want my mama,' cried Needy Neil as Henry trampled on his sleeping bag.

'But I want to marry with you, Henwy,' lisped Lily, trying to follow him.

'Henry! Stay still!' barked Miss Battle-Axe, glaring at him with her demon eyes.

'Hello boys and girls, what an adventure we're going to have tonight,' said the museum's guide, Earnest Ella, as she handed out pencils and worksheets.

Henry groaned. Boring! He hated worksheets.

'Did you know that our museum has a famous collection of balls of wool through the ages?' droned Earnest Ella. 'And an old railway car? Oh yes, it's going to be an exciting sleepover night. We're even going on a torch-lit walk through the corridors.'

Horrid Henry yawned and sneaked a peek at his comic book, which he'd hidden beneath his museum worksheet.

Horrid Henry gasped as he read *How to Recognise a Vampire* and *How to Recognise a Zombie.*

Big scary teeth?

Big googly eyes?

Looks like the walking dead?

Wow, that described Miss Battle-Axe perfectly. All they had to add was big fat carrot nose and . . .

A dark shadow loomed over him.

Chapter 3

'I'll take that,' snapped Miss Battle-Axe, yanking the comic out of his hand. '*And* the rest.'

Huh? He'd been so careful. How had she spotted that comic under his worksheet? And how did she know about the secret stash in his bag?

Horrid Henry looked round the hall. Aha! There was Peter, pretending not to look at him. How dare that wormy worm toad tell on him?

Just for that . . .

'Come along everyone, line up to collect your torches for our spooky walk,' said Earnest Ella. 'You wouldn't want to get left behind in the dark, would you?'

There was no time to lose. Horrid Henry slipped over to Peter's class and joined him in line with Tidy Ted and Goody Goody Gordon.

'Hello Peter,' said Henry sweetly.

Peter looked at him nervously. Did Henry suspect *he'd* told on him? Henry didn't *look* angry.

'Shame my comic got confiscated,' said Henry, "'cause it had a list of how to tell whether anyone you know is a zombie vampire.'

'A zombie vampire?' said Tidy Ted.

'Yup,' said Henry.

'They're imaginary,' said Goody-Goody Gordon.

'That's what they'd *like* you to believe,' said Henry. 'But I've discovered some.'

'Where?' said Ted.

Horrid Henry looked around dramatically, then dropped his voice to a whisper.

'Two teachers at our school,' hissed Henry.

Chapter 4

'Two *teachers*?' said Peter.

'What?' said Ted.

'You heard me. Zombie Vampires. Miss Battle-Axe *and* Miss Lovely.'

'Miss *Lovely*?' gasped Peter.

'You're just making that up,' said Gordon.

'It was all in *Screamin' Demon*,' said Henry. 'That's why Miss Battle-Axe snatched my comic. To stop me finding out the truth. Listen carefully.'

Henry recited:

How to recognise a vampire:
1. BIG HUGE SCARY TEETH.

'If Miss Battle-Axe's fangs were any bigger she would trip over them,' said Horrid Henry.

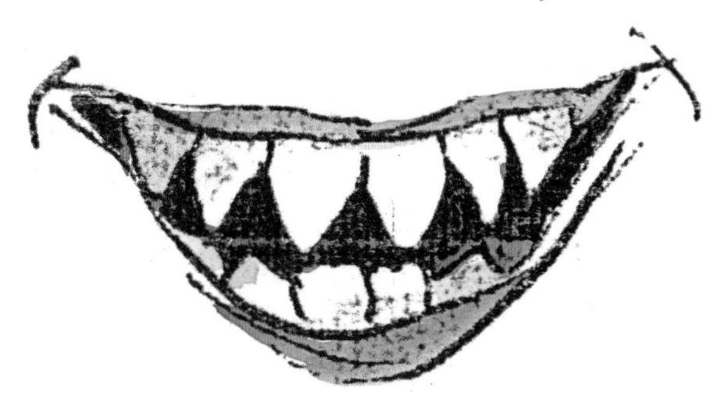

Tidy Ted nodded. 'She *does* have big pointy teeth.'

'That doesn't prove anything,' said Peter.

2. DRINKS BLOOD.

Perfect Peter shook his head. 'Drinks . . . blood?'

'*Obviously* they do, just not *in front* of people,' said Horrid Henry. 'That would give away their terrible secret.'

3. ONLY APPEARS AT NIGHT.

'But Henry,' said Goody-Goody Gordon, 'we see Miss Battle-Axe and Miss Lovely every day at school. They *can't* be vampires.'

Henry sighed. 'Have you been paying attention? I didn't say they were *vampires*, I said they were *zombie* vampires. Being half-zombie lets them walk about in daylight.'

Perfect Peter and Goody-Goody Gordon looked at one another.

'Here's the total proof,'
Henry continued.

How to recognise a zombie:
1. LOOKS DEAD.

'Does Miss Battle-Axe look dead?
Definitely,' said Horrid Henry.
'I never saw a more
dead-looking person.

'But Henry,' said Peter. 'She's alive.'

Unfortunately, yes, thought Horrid Henry. 'Duh,' he said. 'Zombies always *seem* alive. Plus, zombies have got scary, bulging eyes like Miss Battle-Axe,' continued Henry. 'And they feed on human flesh.'

'Miss Lovely doesn't eat human flesh,' said Peter. 'She's a vegetarian.'

'A likely story,' said Henry.

'You're just trying to scare us,' said Peter.

'Don't you see?' said Henry. 'They're planning to pounce on us during the torch-lit trail.'

'I don't believe you,' said Peter.

Henry shrugged. 'Fine. Don't believe me. Just don't say I didn't warn you when Miss Lovely lurches out of the dark and BITES you!' he shrieked.

'Be quiet, Henry,' shouted Miss Battle-Axe. 'William. Stop weeping. There's nothing to be scared of. Linda! Stand up. It's not bedtime yet. Bert! Where's your torch?'

'I dunno,' said Beefy Bert.

Miss Lovely walked over and smiled at Peter. 'Looking forward to the torchlit walk?' she beamed.

Peter couldn't stop himself sneaking a peek at her teeth. *Were* they big? And sharp? Funny, he'd never noticed before how pointy two of them were . . . And was her face a bit . . . umm . . . pale?
No! Henry was just trying to trick him. Well, he wasn't going to be fooled.

'Time to go exploring,' said Earnest Ella.

'First stop on the torch-lit trail: our brand-new exhibit, *Wonderful World of Wool.* Then we'll be popping next door down the *Passage to the Past* to visit the old railway car and the Victorian shop and a Neanderthal cave.

Torches on, everyone.’

Chapter 5

Sour Susan smiled to herself. She'd just thought of the perfect revenge on Margaret for teasing her for being such a scaredy cat.

Moody Margaret smiled to herself. She'd just thought of the perfect revenge on Susan for being so sour.

Ha ha Margaret, thought Susan. I'll get you tonight.

Ha ha Susan, thought Margaret. I'll get you tonight.

Ha ha Peter, thought Henry. I'll get you tonight.

'Follow me,' said Earnest Ella. The children stampeded after her. All except three.

When the coast was clear, Moody Margaret turned off her torch, darted into the pitch-black *Passage to the Past* hall and hid in the Neanderthal cave behind the caveman. She'd leap out at Susan when she walked past.

MWAHAHAHAHAHAHAHA!

Wouldn't that old scaredy cat get a fright.

Sour Susan turned off her torch and peeked down the *Passage to the Past* corridor. Empty. She tiptoed to the railway car and crept inside. Just wait till Margaret walked by . . .

Horrid Henry turned off his torch, crept down the *Passage to the Past*, sneaked into the Victorian shop and hid behind the rocking chair. Tee hee. Just wait till Peter walked past. He'd—

What was that?

Was it his imagination? Or did that spinning wheel in the corner of the shop . . . move?

CR—EEEK went the wheel.

It was so dark. But Henry didn't dare switch on his torch.

Moody Margaret looked over from the Neaderthal cave at the Victorian shop. Was it her imagination or was that rocking chair rocking back and forth?

Sour Susan looked out from the railway car. Was it her imagination or was the caveman moving? There was a strange, scuttling noise. What was that? thought Susan.

You know, thought Henry, this museum *is* kind of creepy at night. And then something grabbed onto his leg.

'AAAARRRRRGGHHH!' screamed Horrid Henry.

Chapter 6

Moody Margaret heard a blood-curdling scream. Scarcely daring to breathe, Margaret peeped over the caveman's shoulder . . .

Sour Susan heard a blood-curdling scream. Scarcely daring to breathe, Susan peeped out from the railway carriage . . .

'Henwy, I found you, Henwy,' piped the creature clinging to his leg.

'Go away Lily,' hissed Henry. The horrible fiend was going to ruin everything.

'Will you marry me, Henwy?'

'No!' said Horrid Henry, trying to shake her off and brushing against the spinning wheel.

CR—EEEEK.

The spinning wheel spun.

What's that noise? thought Margaret, craning to see from behind the caveman.

'Henwy! I want to give you a big kiss,' lisped Lily.

Horrid Henry shook his leg harder. The spinning wheel tottered and fell over.

CRASH!

Margaret and Susan saw something lurch out of the Victorian shop and loom up in the darkness. A monstrous creature with four legs and waving arms…

'AAAARRRRGGHH!'
screamed Susan.

'AAAARGGHHHHH!'
shrieked Margaret.

'AAAARGGHHHHH!'
shrieked Henry.

The unearthly screams rang through the museum. Peter, Ted, and Gordon froze.

'You don't think—' gasped Gordon.

'Not . . . ' trembled Peter.

'Zombie vampires?' whimpered Ted.

They clutched one another.

'Everyone head back to the Central Hall NOW!' shouted Earnest Ella.

In the cafeteria, Miss Lovely and Miss Battle-Axe were snatching a short break to enjoy a lovely fried egg sandwich with lashings of ketchup.

Oh my weary bones, thought Miss Battle-Axe, as she sank her teeth into the huge sandwich. Peace at last.

AAARRGGHH!

EEEEEKKK!

HELLLP!

Miss Battle-Axe and Miss Lovely squeezed their sandwiches in shock as they heard the terrible screams.

SPLAT!

A stream of ketchup squirted Miss Lovely in the eye and dripped down her face onto her blouse.

SQUIRT!

A blob of ketchup splatted Miss Battle-Axe on the nose and dribbled down her chin onto her cardigan.

'Sorry, Boudicca,' said Miss Lovely.

'Sorry, Lydia,' said Miss Battle-Axe.

They raced into the dark Central Hall just as their classes ran back from the torch-lit walk. Fifty beams of light from fifty torches lit up the teachers' ketchup-covered faces and ketchup-stained clothes.

'AAAARRGGHHH!'
screamed Perfect Peter.

'It's the zombie vampires!'
howled Tidy Ted.

'Run for your lives!' yelped
Goody-Goody Gordon.

'Wait!' shouted Miss Lovely! 'Children, come back!'

'We won't eat you!' shouted Miss Battle-Axe.

'AAAARRRRRGGHHHHH!'